T0159328

For my Dad

For information: Notable Kids Publishing www.notablekidspublishing.com
Library of Congress Control Number: 2 0 1 7 9 0 4 7 3 8

Widerøe, Debra L.
The Adventures of Camellia N. – Under the Sea / Book 2 / written by Debra L. Widerøe - 1st Edition
Summary: The Adventures of Camellia N. is the second in a series of nine educational fiction books targeted to children ages 5-9.

Camellia's nightly dreams take her on adventures to all seven continents, under the sea and into space where she learns about and gains appreciation for the environment surrounding her. The second book takes Camellia and her readers on an exciting journey under the sea.

ISBN 9780997085136
Children's Picture Book (Juvenille Fiction 5-9)
Notable Kids Publishing • PO Box 2047, Parker Colorado
Printed in the USA

The Adventures of Camellia N.

Under the Sea

This book belongs to:

Written by **Debra L. Widerøe**   Illustrated by **Daniela Frongia**

Notable Kids Publishing
Printed in the USA

"Who is going with you on your **adventure** tonight, Camellia N.?" her father asked in his warm voice. "Kiwi and Flippy are coming with me. I just can't wait! Good night, Daddy. I love you so."

"Sweet dreams, little Camellia N.
Sleep tight and **safe travels** to you all."
Camellia yawned aloud, and closed her eyes
as the moonlight lit up her room.

"Camellia N. here reporting for service,"
Camellia said confidently to the strange fish staring back at her.
"Am I in a fish bowl?" she asked the polka dot fish.

"Am I also underwater, Mr.Fish?"

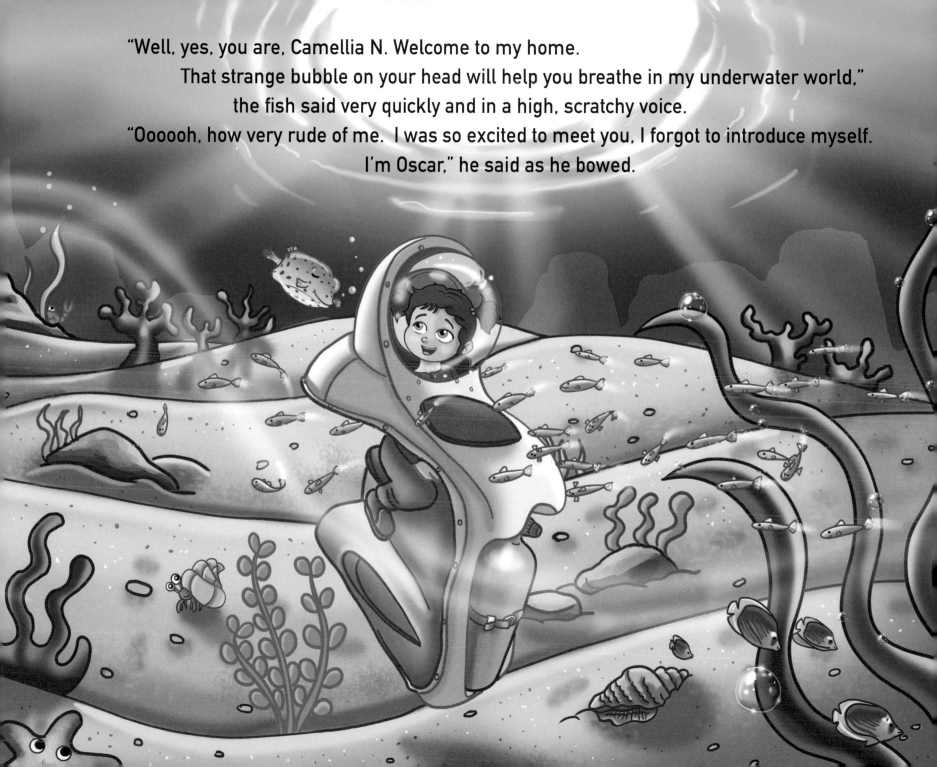

"Well, yes, you are, Camellia N. Welcome to my home.
That strange bubble on your head will help you breathe in my underwater world,"
the fish said very quickly and in a high, scratchy voice.
"Oooooh, how very rude of me. I was so excited to meet you, I forgot to introduce myself.
I'm Oscar," he said as he bowed.

"The sea has even more shades of blue than my biggest crayon box!"
she cheered. There were big fish, little fish, bright fish, teeny-tiny fish
and even see-through fish swimming all around.
Out of the corner of her eye,
Camellia caught a glimpse of a speckled,
dark grey turtle, just like her Flippy.

He smiled and waved while gracefully
swimming through the sea.
"This is going to be
my **BEST** adventure ever!"
Camellia said happily

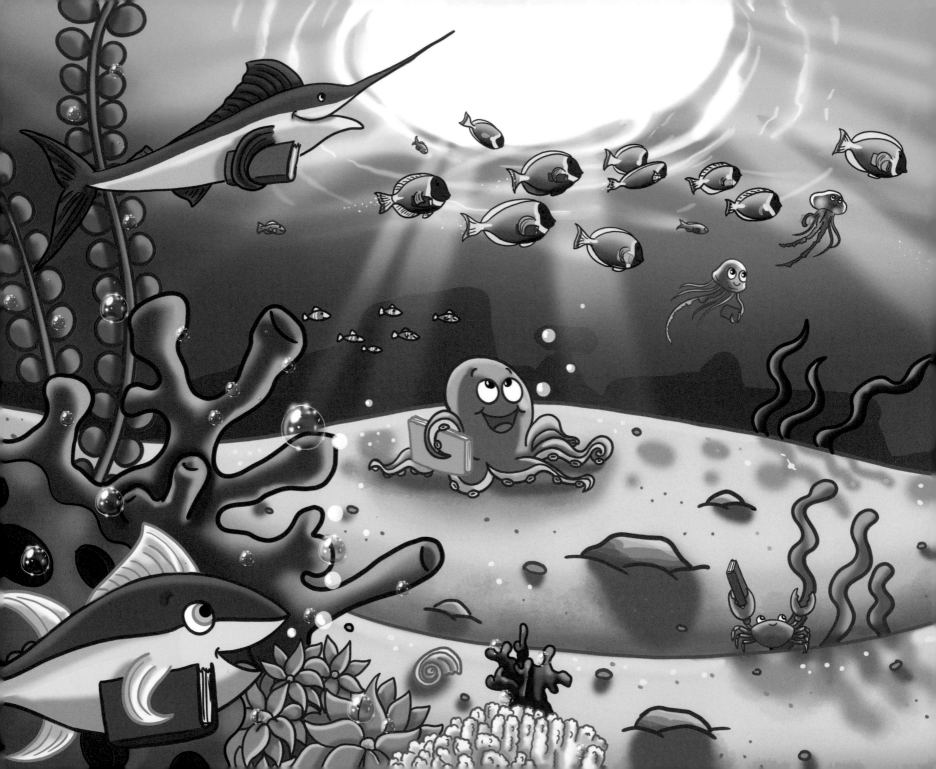

"Well, let's go SEE the SEA, Camellia N.
It's just about school time and we don't want
to be late for school!"
Oscar motioned to Camellia and to all the fish
surrounding them.

"Get your fins moving!"

Oscar shrieked in his high-pitched voice.
Camellia watched with amazement as schools
of fish of all sizes swirled around and then
quickly swam towards school,
just as Oscar asked them to do.

"Now, pay attention little Camellia," Oscar said.
"There is much to learn from the sea.
Follow me and stay very close."

They didn't get far when a **strange** looking sea creature,
with eyes at the side of his head, swam up to them both.
As the large fish came closer, all the smaller fish
seemed to quickly swim away.

The odd fish looked up at Camellia
and then back at Oscar with fear in his eyes.
"Hi Nails," Oscar said sweetly to the shark
as he gave him a "high five" with his fin.
"Uh, don't be scared, Nails.
This is Camellia N. She's my student for the day
on a very special mission to learn about our sea."

Oscar pressed his fish face against the glass surrounding Camellia and said very loudly, "Nails may be very **LARGE** but he's a close buddy of mine. He's a hammerhead, you know." Camellia smiled hesitantly at the large shark.

"Hi Nails. Happy to meet you."

"Nails is a pretty amazing fish, Camellia N." Oscar continued.
"Sharks play an important role in our waters.
Nails sees and smells better than most of us and even knows
who's swimming in the sea nearby.
His head looks just like a hammer, doesn't it?
Well, of course, that's why we call him a hammerhead."

"Although I might be cute and have
polka dots, I'm a simple boxfish.
Nails is SO much more special than I."
Camellia petted his square head gently.
"I think you're just as special, Oscar,
and you're my best fish friend too."
Oscar smiled and
blew her a **kiss**.

"Off to school, my friends," Oscar shrieked.

"I'll ride with Nails. Camellia, you can take the scooter for a spin."

It wasn't long before another large creature caught Camellia's eye.

"Look, Nails and Oscar!"

she said pointing to a big sea creature with long flippers.

Camellia watched as the sweet, dog-faced animal approached her,

tickled her arm with its soft whiskers and passed by. It looked at Camellia and winked sweetly.

With **SQUEEKS** and **ROARS** and **GRUMBLES** and **GRUNTS**,

the animal then swam away so very quickly they didn't even get a chance to meet.

"That was Stella, the stellar sea lion," Oscar squealed. "She's the biggest sea lion and a brand-new mommy, too. You'll see her again as she is quite social." Camellia grinned.

"Look over there, Oscar," Camellia joyfully shouted out. In the distance was a **roly-poly** creature swimming happily upside down.

"That funny looking animal is Ellie. She's a manatee, or **sea cow**, to you and me.
Can you believe she's related to an elephant?" Camellia listened carefully.
"She is an herbivore. Like a vegetarian, she only eats plants."
"Miss Ellie," Oscar called out. "Did you find enough grass and algae today?
You do need your energy for today's class!"
The manatee completely ignored Oscar and continued to swim in her own world,
whistling her favorite tunes.

"That's the funniest
looking animal I've ever seen, Oscar.
But, I don't think Ellie looks like an elephant or a cow!
I'm worried that she's so slow she might not make it
to school on time," Camellia giggled.

The farther they seemed to swim in the sea, the more unusual sea life appeared.
Camellia N. couldn't believe her eyes!
Just before her was a **rainbow-colored** mountain under the sea.

Camellia stared at the underwater trees that swayed as if dancing to music.
Very strange creatures were darting in and out of the bright mountain.
Everything was moving and alive, even the mountain itself.

Camellia moved in even closer and reached out to touch its beautiful branches.

Within a moment, Oscar and Nails swam up, stopping right in front of her with a STOP sign.

"Here's an important lesson for you, missy," Oscar said boldly as he raised a fin and pointed.

"This is OUR coral reef.

Please don't you or anyone dare touch it."

Camellia backed up immediately. "I will never touch your coral reef. I promise you, Oscar."

"Much of our sea life lives here, Camellia N. It's like a city under the sea. Some of us live here all the time, but most of us stop here to rest and play. Without the reefs in our world, most plants and animals wouldn't live," Oscar said seriously, then looked thoughtfully at Camellia.

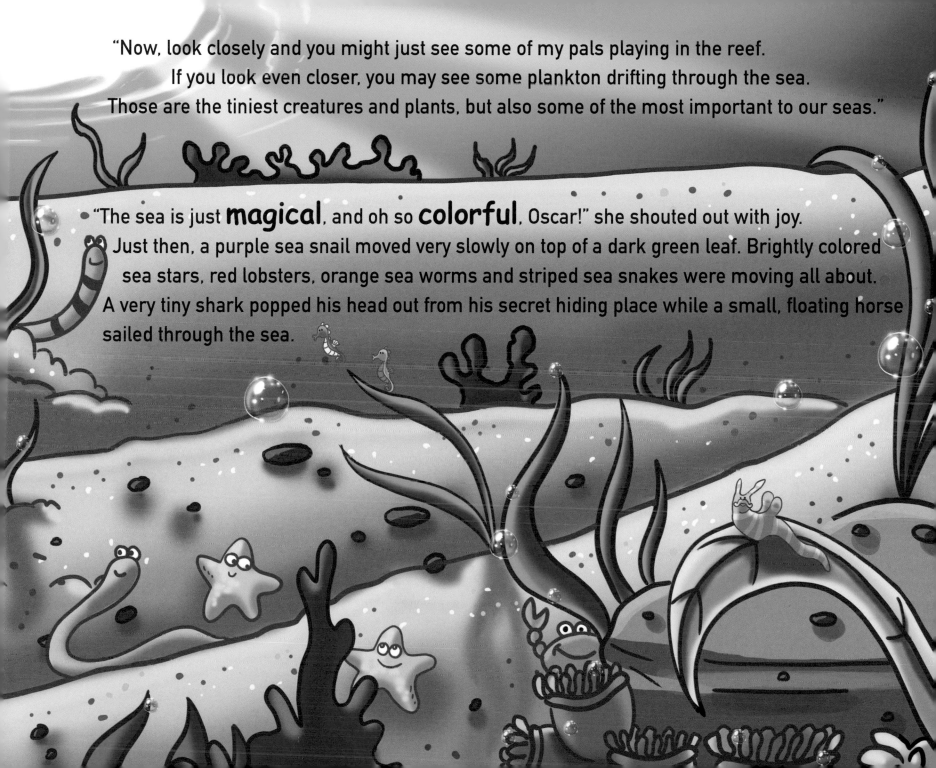

"Now, look closely and you might just see some of my pals playing in the reef.
If you look even closer, you may see some plankton drifting through the sea.
Those are the tiniest creatures and plants, but also some of the most important to our seas."

"The sea is just **magical**, and oh so **colorful**, Oscar!" she shouted out with joy.
Just then, a purple sea snail moved very slowly on top of a dark green leaf. Brightly colored
sea stars, red lobsters, orange sea worms and striped sea snakes were moving all about.
A very tiny shark popped his head out from his secret hiding place while a small, floating horse
sailed through the sea.

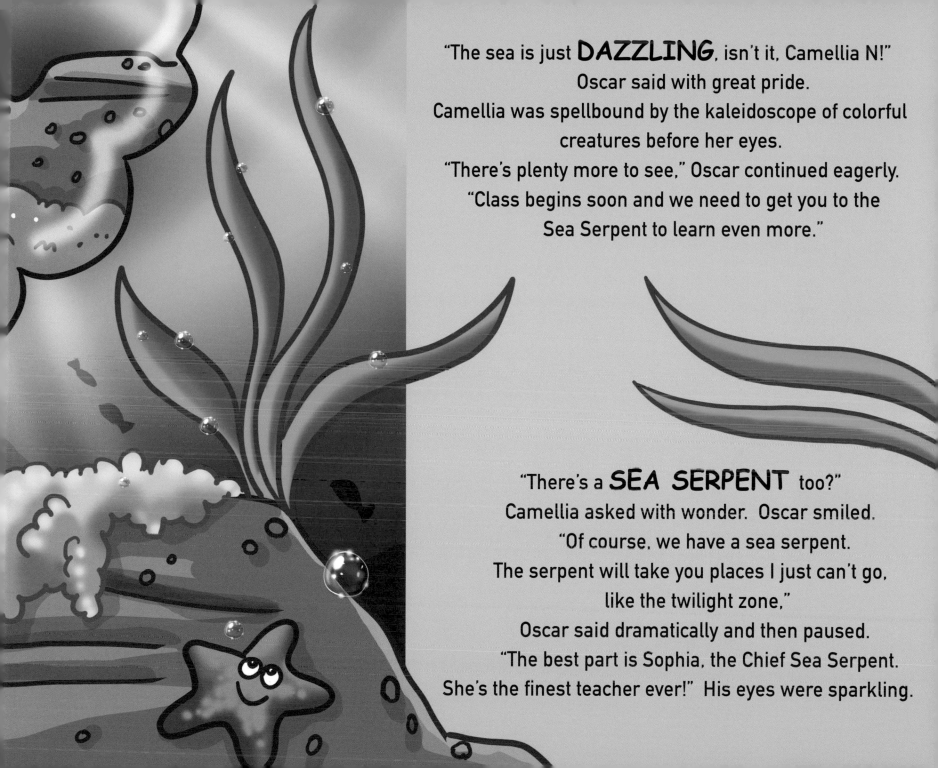

"The sea is just **DAZZLING**, isn't it, Camellia N!"
Oscar said with great pride.
Camellia was spellbound by the kaleidoscope of colorful
creatures before her eyes.
"There's plenty more to see," Oscar continued eagerly.
"Class begins soon and we need to get you to the
Sea Serpent to learn even more."

"There's a **SEA SERPENT** too?"
Camellia asked with wonder. Oscar smiled.
"Of course, we have a sea serpent.
The serpent will take you places I just can't go,
like the twilight zone,"
Oscar said dramatically and then paused.
"The best part is Sophia, the Chief Sea Serpent.
She's the finest teacher ever!" His eyes were sparkling.

"Oh, there she is," Oscar shouted out pointing at the huge gray vessel with the name Sea Serpent. "I'll leave you now, little Camellia N. Enjoy your school in the sea." Oscar and Nails blew bubble kisses and swam away.

"Welcome to the Sea Serpent, little Camellia N. I was expecting you.
This is our **laboratory**, or underwater school in the sea.
I'm the commanding officer and I run this submarine. Please just call me Sophia," said the
light haired woman in her crisp white uniform.

"My team and I are here to explore the sea and show you our special world.
We live, sleep, work and play on the Sea Serpent learning
all about the sea and its many creatures.
I am quite sure Oscar has already shown you his **sunlit zone**,
but there is much more to see.
Come, I'll give you a tour of our submarine first."

Soon Camellia, Sophia and her crew were all together in a very cramped space.
"Clear the bridge!" Sophia said firmly. "We will dive soon." She turned to Camellia and said,
"Are you ready to explore the deep, blue sea, Camellia N.?"
Camellia was so excited she could barely contain her smiles.

Suddenly, the crew started to move quickly pressing all sorts of buttons and pulling
lots of levers. The engine started with a LOUD sound and Camellia heard banging
and clanking as the Sea Serpent began to move.

"We are on our way, Camellia N." Sophia said enthusiastically.
"What are we on our way to, Commander Sophia?"
Camellia asked curiously. "You'll see soon enough, Camellia.
Let's look through our **periscope**, or eye of the serpent,
and begin our first lesson. We will look here as we first dive,
then look outside from a porthole, or window, to you and me."
Camellia ran quickly to the large window to take a peek.

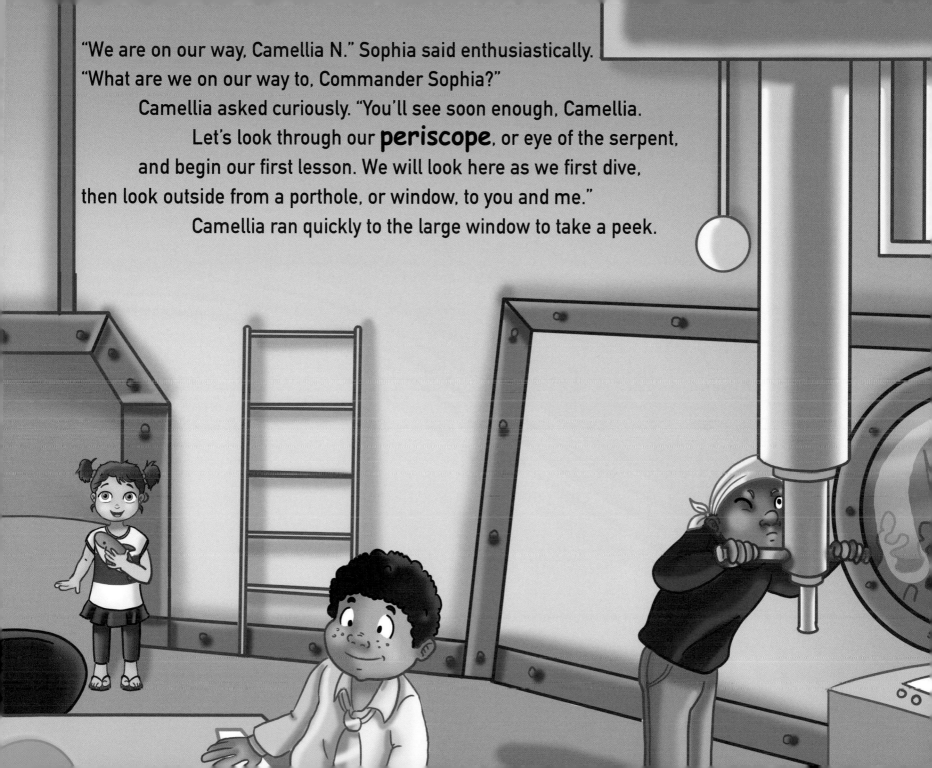

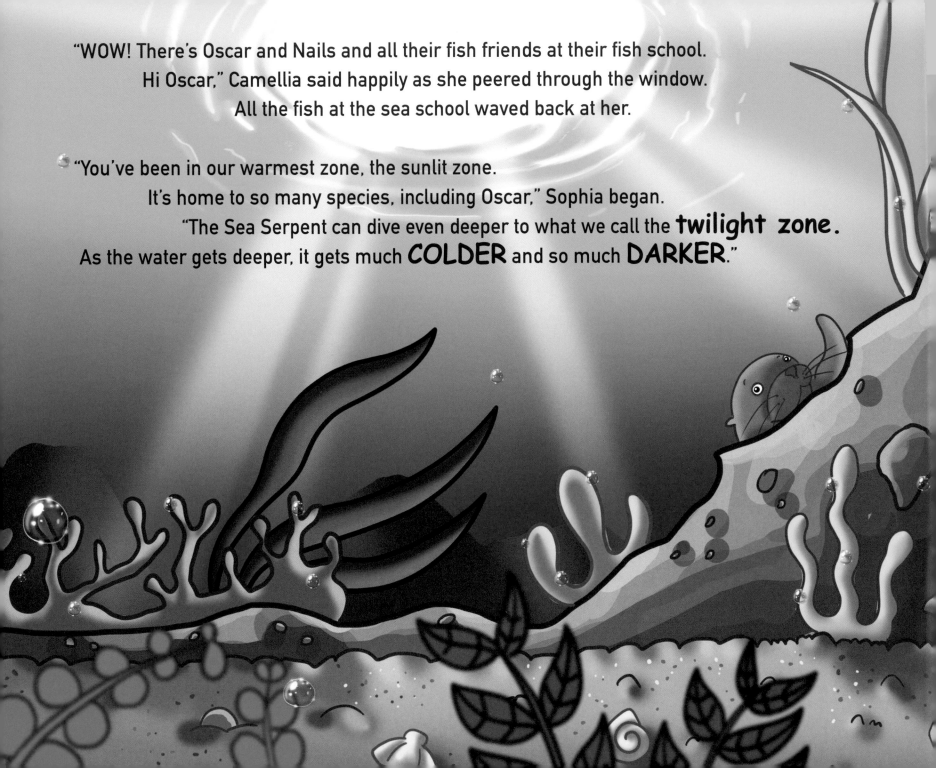

"WOW! There's Oscar and Nails and all their fish friends at their fish school.
Hi Oscar," Camellia said happily as she peered through the window.
All the fish at the sea school waved back at her.

"You've been in our warmest zone, the sunlit zone.
It's home to so many species, including Oscar," Sophia began.
"The Sea Serpent can dive even deeper to what we call the **twilight zone**.
As the water gets deeper, it gets much **COLDER** and so much **DARKER**."

"Look over here, Commander Sophia! I see swarms of baby fish.
There are more fish than my eyes have ever seen."
Camellia was dazzled by the **swarm of fish**, which looked to her just like a fish-filled
beehive, circling right outside the submarine window.

"Keep watching, Camellia! Where there are seas of krill, there will be much larger sea animals."
Camellia kept her eyes glued to the window. Hearing **GROANS** and **MOANS** through the
microphone, she then caught a glimpse of the largest blue-gray creature she had ever seen
coming towards them.

"Come quick, Commander Sophia," Camellia said with excitement.
"I see something so **HUGE** coming so **CLOSE**,
maybe a bit too close to the Sea Serpent.
It's so **GIANT** I can only see a part of it!"
Sophia looked through another porthole and
confirmed what she had expected.
"Ah. I'm so happy you can see our
blue whales on your adventure
with us, Camellia N. Indeed,
this is a very special treat."

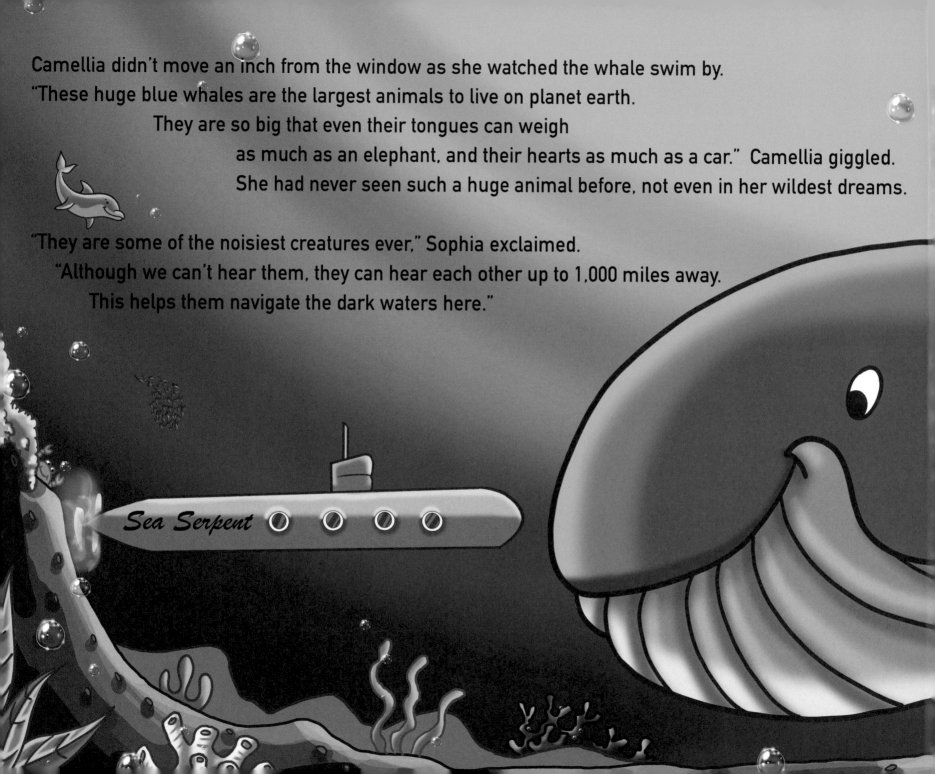

Camellia didn't move an inch from the window as she watched the whale swim by.
"These huge blue whales are the largest animals to live on planet earth.
They are so big that even their tongues can weigh
as much as an elephant, and their hearts as much as a car." Camellia giggled.
She had never seen such a huge animal before, not even in her wildest dreams.

"They are some of the noisiest creatures ever," Sophia exclaimed.
"Although we can't hear them, they can hear each other up to 1,000 miles away.
This helps them navigate the dark waters here."

Sea Serpent

"There are millions of species in the sea and millions
we haven't even learned about yet," explained Sophia.
Strange looking jellyfish were
gently gliding by, alongside porpoises and dolphin,
including one who looked just like her dolphin, Kiwi.

Camellia waved to them as they passed by the window.
"Your little friend, Kiwi, is a Maui Dolphin," Sophia said sweetly.
"Hold onto him very tightly and take especially good care of him.
There are only 55 dolphins like Kiwi left in our sea. It is so very special you got
a chance to see him in the wild." Camellia had a tear in her eye, as she held Kiwi close by her side.

"**Let's dive to the twilight zone,**" shouted Commander Sophia to her crew
as the submarine began to descend farther.
"We will use our lights so you can look outside the window, Camellia.
It's a world not many people get a chance to see."

The engines made a whooshing noise as the submarine dove deep down underwater.
Daytime turned to night, and soon the sea became dark and still.
"Why is everything so dark down here, Commander Sophia?" Camellia asked curiously.

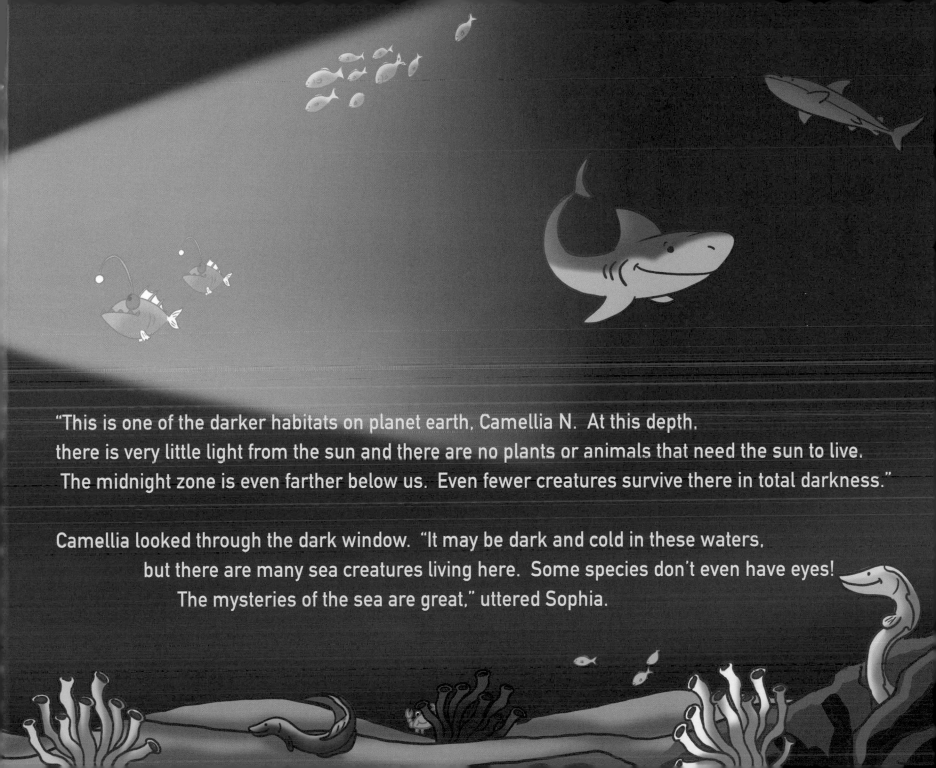

"This is one of the darker habitats on planet earth, Camellia N. At this depth,
there is very little light from the sun and there are no plants or animals that need the sun to live.
The midnight zone is even farther below us. Even fewer creatures survive there in total darkness."

Camellia looked through the dark window. "It may be dark and cold in these waters,
but there are many sea creatures living here. Some species don't even have eyes!
The mysteries of the sea are great," uttered Sophia.

Camellia was fascinated. "Please tell me more, Sophia," she begged.
"Other species in this zone have very large eyes, helping them to see better in these dark waters,"
Sophia said as she pointed outside the window.
"You may notice that most of the animals here are dark themselves to help them hide from prey.
There are even sea creatures that make their own light and seem to glow,
just like that very odd spookfish swimming right outside our window."

Camellia stared outside the window at all the strange sea creatures surrounding her.
The odd **spookfish** was glowing and its see-through head made its eyes look even spookier.

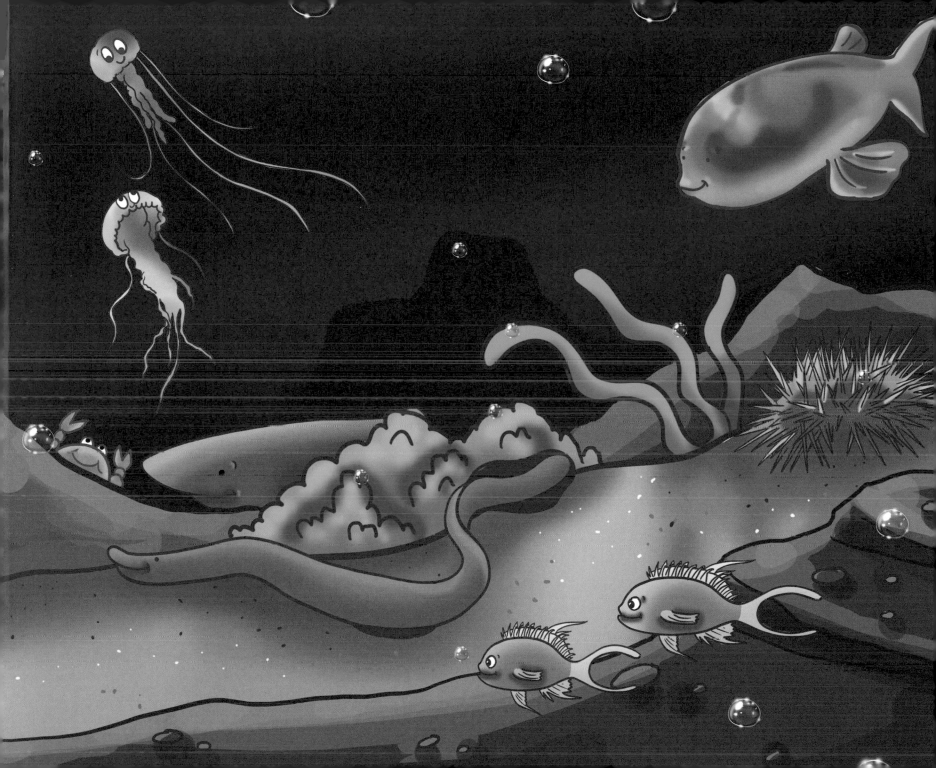

"I want to come back again and again, Commander Sophia,"
Camellia said stifling a yawn, her eyes fighting to stay open.
The darkness had made her quite sleepy.

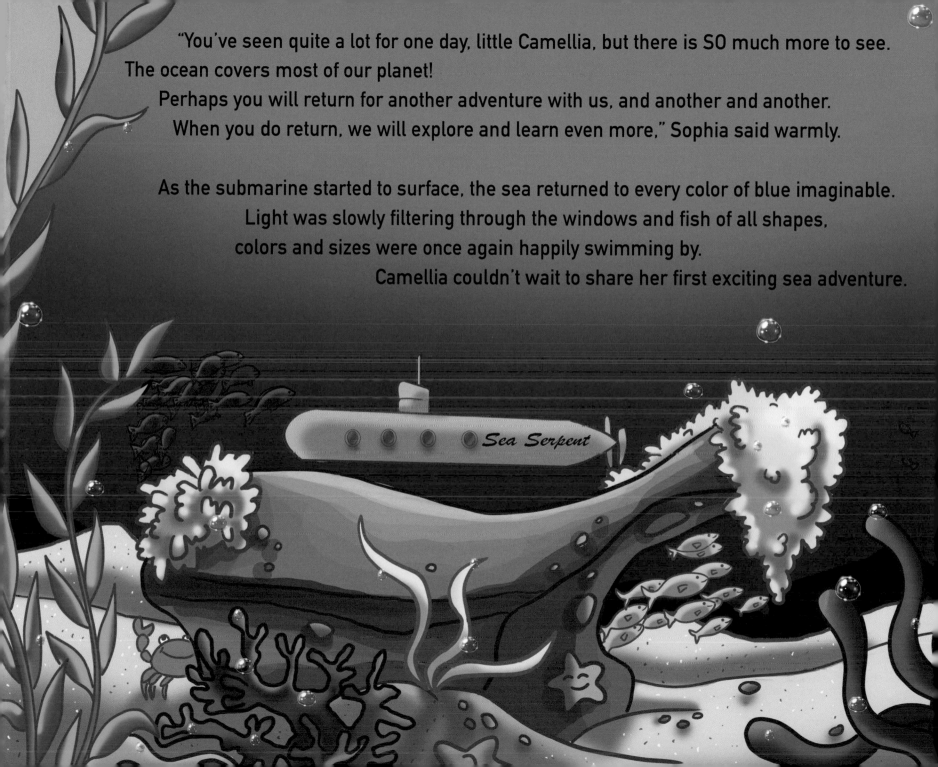

"You've seen quite a lot for one day, little Camellia, but there is SO much more to see.
The ocean covers most of our planet!
Perhaps you will return for another adventure with us, and another and another.
When you do return, we will explore and learn even more," Sophia said warmly.

As the submarine started to surface, the sea returned to every color of blue imaginable.
Light was slowly filtering through the windows and fish of all shapes,
colors and sizes were once again happily swimming by.
Camellia couldn't wait to share her first exciting sea adventure.

Sea Serpent

Under the **deep blue sea**, leatherback turtles were gracefully swimming,
manatees floated upside-down whistling their favorite tunes, Maui dolphins were playing tag,
blue whales were traveling from sea to sea, all while a tiny sea horse sailed
on a magic carpet ride sitting on a single blade of grass.

"The world is more beautiful than I ever imagined. I will treasure it and take care of it forever."

The End